THE STONE MAN MYSTERIES

BOOK THREE

Breaking Out The Devil

JANE YOLEN AND ADAM STEMPLE
ILLUSTRATED BY ORION ZANGARA

GRAPHIC UNIVERSE™ • MINNEAPOLIS

To David Francis Stemple, who knows Edinburgh well enough —JY

For my favorite trilogy: Betsy, Ari, and David —AS

To Katie (my beautiful wife), Lisa and Mark (my wonderful parents), Troy (my incredibly smart brother), and Richard and Sarah (my great in-laws). I couldn't do any of this without you! —OZ

Story by Jane Yolen and Adam Stemple
Illustrations by Orion Zangara
Front cover coloring by Steve Canon
Lettering by Bill Hauser

Graphic Universe™
An imprint of Lerner Publishing Group, Inc.
241 First Avenue North
Minneapolis, MN 55401 USA

For reading levels and more information, look up this title at www.lernerbooks.com.

Main body text set in CCWildWords. Typeface provided by Comicraft.

Library of Congress Cataloging-in-Publication Data

Names: Yolen, Jane, author. | Stemple, Adam, author. | Zangara, Orion, illustrator.
Title: Breaking out the devil / Jane Yolen and Adam Stemple ; illustrated by Orion Zangara.
Description: Minneapolis : Graphic Universe, [2019] | Series: Stone man mysteries ; book three |
    Summary: "Silex and his assistant Craig must prevent one of the Devil's lieutenants from
    overtaking both the underworld and Earth" —Provided by publisher.
Identifiers: LCCN 2018038303 (print) | LCCN 2018043375 (ebook) | ISBN 9781541561151 (eb pdf) |
    ISBN 9781467741989 (lb : alk. paper)
Subjects: LCSH: Graphic novels. | CYAC: Graphic novels. | Gargoyles—Fiction. | Supernatural—
    Fiction. | Demonology—Fiction. | Scotland—History—20th century—Fiction. | Mystery and
    detective stories.
Classification: LCC PZ7.7.Y65 (ebook) | LCC PZ7.7.Y65 Br 2019 (print) | DDC 741.5/973—dc23

LC record available at https://lccn.loc.gov/2018038303

Manufactured in the United States of America
1-36195-16979-5/1/2019

Previously in THE STONE MAN MYSTERIES

Edinburgh, Scotland. The early 1930s. Young Craig, a desperate runaway, goes to the top of a church to throw himself off. But he is saved by a strange stone man, a gargoyle named Silex, who can move and speak but cannot leave the church parapet. Silex runs a detective agency and hires Craig to be his chief clue finder, since his last assistant has departed and the church's priest, Father Harris, is getting old.

Craig is shocked, but he signs on. Together, the gargoyle and the young lad solve the mysterious murder of an earl, as well as the deaths of several street people. But the solution points to a deeper, uglier conspiracy. One that involves freeing the Stone Man from his bonds, which will turn him from a force for good back into the evil demon he once was. In that form, he would threaten not only the church, Edinburgh, and Scotland, but indeed the entire world.

Father Harris gives his life to thwart the conspiracy. But troubles at the church continue. When a girl, Ealasaid—an innocent, yet guilty of a terrible crime—makes her way out of Hell, she begs the church for sanctuary. And a fallen angel comes to return her to the Underworld.

Once again, Craig and Silex push back against the darkness, sending the girl to Heaven with the aid of the new priest, Father Walker. But now the last battle is about to commence.

STAIRS

I WONDERED
HOW LONG HE'D
LAST. THE STONE
MAN CAN BE SUCH
A MONSTER.

ASK THE DEVIL?

WE HAVE A... POINT OF CONTACT. I'D HOPED WE'D NEVER NEED TO USE IT.

MAKE YERSELF READY, BOY. I'LL TELL YE ALL YE NEED TO KNOW AND NAE MORE.

YOU'LL BE ASKING TO SPEAK WITH ROBERT WODDROP...

IT ISNAE SAFE.

HE'S TOO YOUNG.

THERE'S NAE PLACE SAFE WHEN DEMONS WALK THE EARTH.

AND THE YOUNG STILL SEE THINGS THE AULD HAVE LEARNED TO IGNORE.

CHAPTER 2
ASYLUM

Royal Edinburgh Hospital
for Mental
and Nervous Disorders

Royal Edinburgh Hospital
for Mental
and Nervous Disorders

STONE MAN!

ONLY ROBERT COULD ENTER TO VISIT HIS SISTER WITHOUT NEEDING AN EXCUSE.

AND HIS PRESENCE WOULDNAE MAKE A DEMON SUSPICIOUS LIKE A PRIEST'S WOULD.

Edinburgh Home for Young Women

WE'D SET UP ROBERT TO BE A DEMON CATCHER, YE SEE, WITH THAT PENTAGRAM ON HIS BACK.

IF THE DEMON INVOLVED WAS STILL AT THE HOME, THE PENTAGRAM'S WEB WOULD SNARE THE IMP. AT LEAST LONG ENOUGH FOR US TO GET ROBERT AWAY AND TO THE CHURCH, WHERE I COULD GIVE THE DEMON A GOOD THROTTLING.

WEE ROBERT WAS A BRAVE SOUL. NEVER CRIED OUT ONCE DURING THE INKING.

BUT IF WE HAD CAPTURED THE DEMON, IT HAD TAKEN ROBERT CAPTIVE AT THE SAME TIME.

FATHER HARRIS RUSHED IN, BUT...

...HE COULDN'T RETRIEVE THE ROBERT WE KNEW.

WHEN IT WAS OVER, THREE MORE YOUNG WOMEN WERE DEAD OF A STRANGE FIRE IN THE HOME AND ROBERT WAS LOCKED AWAY IN THE MADHOUSE.

HIS SISTER BECAME A WARD OF THE CHURCH, SENT TO A NURSING COLLEGE SO SHE COULD EVENTUALLY CARE FOR HER BROTHER.

CHAPTER 8
A STORM BREWING

WHERE NEXT?

THERE!

WHY NOT BLOW IT DOWN?

TOO DANGEROUS IN A SMALL SPACE...

WHAT ARE YE DOING WITH MY BROTHER, YE LUMMOX?

IT'S ALL RIGHT.

WE'RE THE GOOD LADS. HERE TO SAVE HIM.

THAT BIG ONE DOESNAE LOOK LIKE A GOOD LAD AT ALL.

YOU'LL HAVE TO TRUST ME ON THAT.

CHAPTER 9
THE FINAL BATTLE

KNEEL, MORTALS. KNEEL BEFORE YOUR NEW GOD.

CURSE YOU, BAAL, AND THE HORSE YOU RODE IN ON.

SILEX. I KNEW YOU WOULD COME. HERE WAS NO AY YOU COULD RESIST THIS FIGHT.

ARWLRRRROOOAARR

BREAKING AWAY FROM YOUR CHURCH SEEMS TO HAVE BROUGHT OUT THE DEMON IN SILEX.

NOW'S THE TIME TO SET *ME* LOOSE.

IT'S NAE JUST A DELUSION, IS IT? ALL ALONG, I THOUGHT IT HAD TO BE.

YES. IT'S TRULY THE DEVIL INSIDE YER BROTHER.

gasp!

IT'S MOVED. THE INK HAS MOVED! IT'S ALIVE!

HOW CAN WE SEVER THE CONNECTION AND GET ROBBIE BACK?

FAREWELL, LAD.

sigh.

I SUPPOSE I'LL HAVE TO FIND ANOTHER BOY OR ELSE CLOSE UP SHOP.

I EXPECT YOU, PRIEST, WOULD PREFER IT IF I RETIRED.

WHY SHOUD YOU RETIRE? AS CRAIG SAID, WE NEED YOU.

YOU DENIED THE DEVIL HIS DUE. WHO BETTER TO KEEP SAVING US?